Be sure to follow us!

Subscribe to:

Instagram@thegolfdiaries

FB@thegolfdiaries

Twitter@thegolfdiaries

YouTube@TheGolfDiariesGirl

Contact us at gwen@thegolfdiaries.com for information on bulk purchases or speaking engagements. The Golf Diaries can bring the author to your live event.

Good

Smooches

Putt

Excited

Love

Goofy

Not sure

Happy

Fun

The

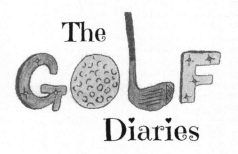

GOLF

Diaries

www.thegolfdiaries.com

Paw Pal's

Gwen Elizabeth Foddrell

Throughout the book are underlined golf tips and terms.

Illustrations by Ginger, Gwen, Jeff and Will. Characters by Alphonzo Rodwell. Cover design by Gwen Foddrell.

For information on special discounts or bulk pricing contact www.thegolfdiaires.com or email at gwen@thegolfdiaries.com

ISBN-13 9781522779667
ISBN-10 1522779663

This Diary belong to

Chloe Castleberry

a friend of _____

June 1

I. Am. Freaking. Out!!!!

My parents finally said "YES" to Caleb and I getting a dog!

I can't believe it!!

SQUEEEEEEE!!!!!!!!!!!

All I can do is think about how much fun it is going to be to take my dog

on the golf course and have her walk
around with me as I play golf!

I don't know how or when I will get
my dog.

I feel an intense urgency to get her
ASAP because I am afraid my parents
might change their mind. And, if they
did...I would be devastated!

Logically, I know they wouldn't do
that, but I am so freaked out that
they actually said, "Yes."

I feel like I need to hurry up and get
her picked out before they change
their minds.

Every night when I go to sleep I
wonder what my dog will look like.

I can't wait for my dog to sleep with
me, go on walks with me, and play golf
with me! My life will be so perfect
once I get my dog.

I did A TON of research on what kind
of dog would be the best dog for our
family.

My research said the number one dog
choice for our family would be a
Boston Terrier.

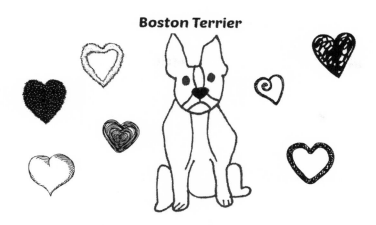

Boston Terrier

It said Boston Terriers don't require grooming, they adapt to their owner's activity level, they don't require a big yard, and they are very gentle with kids and older people.

This WILL BE the PERFECT DOG for us!

In addition to getting a dog I am also still waiting on my new golf clubs to come in.

My mom ordered them for me with the money I earned from selling my figure skating stuff on EBay.

She ordered them from the Palm Woods Country Club (PWCC) pro-shop.

They are just like the ones Tyler gave my brother to use.

I can't wait for them to come in! I know I am going to play better with them.

I am so excited to have my new clubs! My new dog! AND...I. Think. My new GBF (Golf Boyfriend).

At the moment, my life could not be going ANY better!

Well, except for one thing.

My relationship with Mackenzie! I think she is kind of okay with me liking Tyler but I am not sure.

She gives me harsh looks sometimes and asks me interrogating questions that I try to avoid.

I want to keep from having conflict with her.

Mackenzie is the best female golfer at PWCC, and Tyler is the best male golfer at PWCC. I know she thinks they would make the perfect couple.

I really like Mackenzie. I love playing with her because she can be so funny, and she really IS a good golfer!

I want her to like me...I just hope she is okay with ME liking Tyler.

I know she has visions of herself being with Tyler, but I don't think he shares her same feelings.

At least that is what his sister Tessa tells me.

She tells me he avoids her and finds her bossy, demanding, and annoying.

A few weeks ago, when Mackenzie saw me playing in the youth scramble with Tyler, Tessa, and Caleb, I wasn't sure if she was ever going to talk to me again.

She kept giving me the most awful looks.

It kind of scared me!

Maybe once I get my dog and my new golf clubs, she and I can go play golf together and take my dog along with us.

I know she loves dogs, too. We really do have a lot in common.

I love that Mackenzie is a girly girl like I am.

She loves animals, pink, and oh yeah...Tyler!!

Okay, maybe we have a little too much in common...LOL.

Well, I will use my little doggie to try to make her forget about Tyler.

Fingers crossed!!

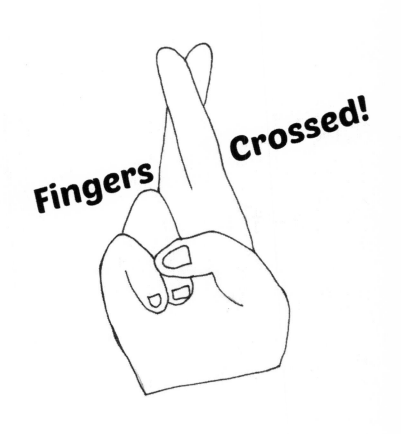

June 2

SQUUUUUEEEEEEEE!!!!!!!

My mom called from work and gave me the most amazing news today!

She said the PWCC pro shop called her and my clubs came in.

I. Am. So. Excited!!!!

I can hardly wait until we go pick them up!

As soon as my mom got home from work I asked her right away if we could go over and get them.

She said yes, but we didn't leave right away.

I waited for about 5 minutes, and I then asked her again if we could PLEASE go over NOW to pick them up.

She said, "Hold on, Chloe, no one will take them. They were a special order for you. We will go after we eat something. I don't want to go over there hungry!"

She continued getting out sandwich makings so we could make some lunch before we went over to the club.

I was so excited I could barely eat my sandwich.

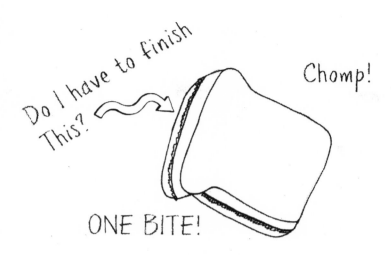

I chewed fast, finished quickly, and rushed to the garage.

We finally got in our golf cart and headed toward the club.

As we were approaching the club we ran into Mackenzie and her mom in their golf cart.

My mom and I both waved, and Mrs. Maureen put her hand up for us to stop.

We stopped and Mackenzie said, "Chloe, where are you going?"

I could tell by the tone in her voice that today she was feeling like bossy Mackenzie, but I answered her anyway.

I told her I had ordered some new golf clubs, and we were going to pick them up in the clubhouse.

She swiftly asked, "What kind did you get?"

I didn't dare tell her that they were like the ones Tyler gave Caleb...I do NOT need to mention TYLER'S NAME around her AT ALL if I can help it!

I just told her they were the US KIDS clubs and they were the 60's, which meant they were for kids who are around 60 inches tall.

She said, "After you pick them up, meet me on the range and we can hit balls together."

I looked at my mom, and she nodded and said, "Sure, I can drop you off at the range."

Mackenzie heads on over to the range and I have this awful feeling. I start thinking she is going to drill me on questions about Tyler.

I have to come up with a plan to avoid talking about him AT ALL with her, but if she asks me directly about him...I am sticking with DIVERSION!!!!!!!! I am going to divert her to another topic...Dogs!

I walk into the club and the head pro has my box ready behind the counter.

SQUEEEEE!!!!!!

He hands them to me, and as I look in the box...they look AMAZING!!!

They also came with a new bag.

I had no idea I was also getting a new bag!

I tear the box open right in the shop and set them in front of the counter.

They look AMAZING!

I bolt from the pro shop and head over to the range to meet Mackenzie.

I can't wait to hit them!

I get on the range and Mackenzie has saved me a spot right by her. I nervously start hitting balls…OMG!!! I am hitting them so good!!!!

I am so excited!

They are just the right size for me, and I notice right away that they are not heavy at all.

Even Mackenzie's eyebrows are a little raised at how well I am striking the ball.

I am hoping that she is so preoccupied with watching me hit shots that she forgets to mention Tyler.

Next thing I know, she point blank asks me, in a very strong voice, "So, do you like Tyler?"

I am so thrown by her question I totally forget my tactic of diversion.

I pause, and pause, and pause. I'm not sure how to answer, because I know what she means, but I also know what I want her to think.

I think about it, and in a nonchalant way reply, "Sure I do, don't you?"

She says, "DUH!!! EVERYONE knows I like him!"

I give a little laugh and ask her if she wants to try and hit one of my new clubs. I keep thinking...DIVERSION, DIVERSION, DIVERSION!!

Her face lights up. She picks one up and we are back to hitting balls.

Whew! That went better than I thought!

I need to keep talking about my clubs and my soon to have new dog, and keep her off of the "Tyler Train"!

June 3

I always like to make sure I am looking "Blingtastic" before I head to the golf course.

I mean, I know I am guaranteed to see lots of people, and most importantly, Tyler! So I have to make sure I am always looking my best!

Caleb gets tired of waiting on me to get dressed, and today is no exception.

When he gets tired of waiting, he walks on over by himself and starts practicing while I finish up getting dressed. Since we live on the golf course it only takes 5 minutes to walk over.

Today as I was walking over to the club I was thinking about how I would probably go to the range first to hit some balls with my new clubs.

Until...I see CALEB and TYLER playing a putting game on the practice putting green.

The game they are playing is one I play with Caleb sometimes. It is called Battleship.

In this game they are each standing by a hole on the practice green, across from each other. Then they see who can make 11 putts first. They both hit their putts at the same time. Whoever sinks their putt gets a point and after someone reaches 5 you switch sides. The first one to 11 wins.

After seeing them on the putting green I change my mind...I decide to go putt first.

As I walk up to them Tyler says, "Hey Chloe, Caleb was telling me your parents said 'yes' to you both getting a dog. That is awesome!"

I grin and reply, "I know! I can't believe it! I want to hurry up and find a dog before they change their mind!"

Tyler says, "Chloe, on Thursdays I volunteer at the Paw Pals animal shelter right outside the country club. It is locally owned, so it is small, but I am sure they wouldn't mind if you came with me this Thursday. You might find a dog there that you really like and your parents would let you have. There are SO many cute dogs there!"

I want to SCREAM! YES, YES, YES!!!!! But instead, in my most calm voice I answer, "That sounds great!"

How did I NOT know he volunteered at an animal shelter!!!!! TYLER IS BEYOND PERFECT!

He is the most amazing golfer, has a perfect smile, says the sweetest things, and is soooooo good looking!!! I could stare into his brown eyes all day!

Still trying to act calm, even though I am freaking out inside, I told him, "I will check with my mom and let you know."

But in my head I am thinking THERE IS NO WAY I AM NOT GOING!!!

I am flipping out that he asked me to go to the animal shelter with him!

I am trying to remain calm and seem unaffected, so I asked him, in my calm, nonchalant voice, "What time on Thursdays do you go?"

Tyler told me he goes in the afternoon.

He said even though school is out he keeps the same schedule year round.

He said he would see if his mom would pick me up on the way and we can go together. I replied, "Cool! I will text you as soon as I talk to my mom to see if I can go."

OKAY, I AM FREAKING OUT AND ALL I WANT TO DO IS SCREAM!!!!

Now I start thinking...I get to go play with adorable dogs this week, and one could potentially be mine. And, TYLER ASKED ME TO GO WITH HIM!!!!

I mean, is this a date???

I didn't think it was, but maybe it is??

My mind is going crazy, and I start adding things up in my head.

1. He told Caleb he has a girlfriend.
2. I would think his girlfriend would not be happy with him inviting me to go to the dog shelter with him.
3. He did invite me to play in the scramble with him...well him, Caleb, and Tessa.

4. He also came and watched my bunny in the church talent show.

I would think that if he had a girlfriend she would not be happy with him inviting me to do all these things with him.

I have got to find out if I AM his GIRLFRIEND, or should I say his GGF (Golf Girlfriend)!!!!

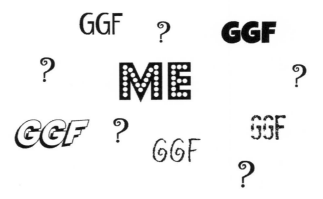

I had tried before to put Caleb on the task of finding out the "deets", but this is what he found out...Yes, he does have a girlfriend. THAT'S IT!!! He didn't follow up with the next question, which was the most important question...

"WHO IS YOUR GIRLFRIEND?"

Caleb told me that when he asked Tyler if he had a girlfriend, he just laughed and said, "Uh, Yeah!"

This could mean a thousand things:

...Uh yeah, none of your business, because you are younger than me.

...Uh yeah, why wouldn't I have a girlfriend? Look at me!

...Uh yeah, you have seen her and didn't know it!

AND LAST BUT NOT LEAST...

...Uh yeah, IT IS YOUR SISTER!!!
I AM HOPING IT IS THE LAST ONE
BECAUSE THAT WOULD MEAN TYLER
IS MY GBF (Golf Boyfriend)!!! I'm
DYING TO FIND OUT!!!

I CAN'T TAKE THE SUSPENSE!!! I
MUST FIND OUT!!

June 4

Today is Saturday, and it is my next-door neighbor's birthday!

She is a year younger than me, but we hang out together and play in the neighborhood a couple of times a week.

She knows how bad I want a dog because I talk about wanting one ALL THE TIME!

It is 8 o'clock in the morning and I hear a knock at our front door.

I hate getting out of bed early on Saturdays, because on Saturday, if we have a golf tournament, they always give us afternoon tee times.

I like to be well rested, and sleeping late helps that!

I know we don't have a tournament today, but I still like to sleep in when I can!

I throw on some clothes and am on my way to the door. Just as I get to the top of our steps, I hear the knock again.

I head down the steps, and I can see through the oval glass in the door that it is Samantha, which is weird FOR HER on a Saturday...she always sleeps in too!

I open the door and Samantha is holding a fluffy little puppy!

She is squealing and jumping up and down.

Her puppy is all dressed up with a birthday hat and a fluffy party dress.

I ask her, "Did you get a new puppy?"

She said, "YEP! I SURE DID! FOR MY BIRTHDAY!"

I tell her, "Happy Birthday and Congratulations."

I was trying to smile and look and sound happy for her, but it is 8 O'CLOCK ON A SATURDAY!!!

And on top of that, I am the one who always talks about wanting a dog.

I have never heard her once say she wanted a dog.

I think she got one because she knew I wanted one!

She has never even seemed interested in the dogs around the neighborhood when we have been playing outside.

I asked her what her puppy's name was and she replied, "Her name is Fluffy."

I bend down to pet her puppy. She is a super cute little dog that is white

in color and SO FLUFFY all over;
Fluffy is a perfect name for her!
She then told me, "She is only 8
weeks old."

Fluffy kept licking me, and I felt like
she really seemed to like me!

I couldn't help but wish she were
mine!

 Why can't I have a sweet puppy now?

She said that she had to take her to
the vet for a checkup this morning

and she would be back later...she just wanted ME to SEE HER DOG!

I said that maybe we could play later, after she took her to the vet.

She said, "Sure, sounds good." She walked away with the biggest grin on her face and bounced down from the steps of our front door with her adorable puppy all dressed in cute clothes.

I just couldn't stop thinking about HER actually having a dog!

I went back to bed and I was hoping it was all a dream. I was hoping it was a dream mix up, and that the cute little dog Fluffy was really mine!

I feel like screaming inside because I AM THE ONE THAT WANTS A DOG!!!!

If I had just received a dog as a gift, I would be jumping up and down and doing cartwheels because I would be sooooo happy!!!!

So I guess I can understand HER being so happy.

After she took Fluffy to the vet she came back over to my house and wanted to know if I could go on a walk with her.

I said, "YES, that would be great!"

So we took Fluffy on a walk. She is a sweet and smart little dog!

I wish I could have a turn!

I just wish she were MY DOG!

As we started to walk Fluffy, she kept tripping on the leash.

I said, "Samantha, maybe the leash is too long. Try to hold it shorter so Fluffy won't keep tripping."

I bent down and untangled the leash and the leash dropped on the ground.

47

I picked it up and asked Samantha if I could have a turn walking her.

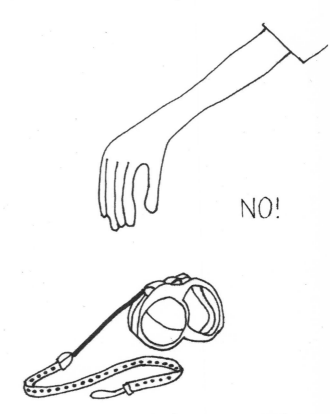

NO!

She snatched the leash from me and said, "NO!"

I was surprised she wouldn't let me have a turn walking the dog.

I was really hurt she wouldn't share the fun with me!

We started walking again and she started talking about how amazing HER dog is and HER dog is so perfect...even the veterinarian said so!

She then started talking about all the cute things she got to go with HER dog.

She said she got a pajama set for nighttime, squeaky toys to play with, and a cute princess bed.

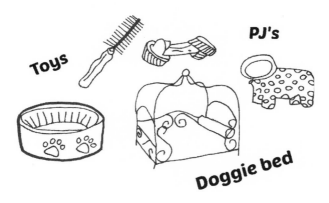

Toys

PJ's

Doggie bed

She kept going on and on about how perfect everything was!

I would literally die if I got a dog and all that stuff!

I was feeling so hurt that I didn't have a dog...then you add the tone of her voice when she was talking about HER dog, and it seemed like she was rubbing it in my face that she had a puppy and I didn't.

By the end of the walk I could barely hold back my tears.

I couldn't wait to get home because I wanted to go to my room and cry!

Before I walked back in my house she then asked me, " Do you want to go to the movies with me for my birthday this afternoon?"

I told her I would ask my mom and text her.

AS I walk in my house I shut the door quickly because I needed to get away from her for the moment.

She was gloating about her dog and acting like she was better than me. She wouldn't even let me have a turn to hold the leash.

I couldn't take it anymore!!

Because honestly, her having a dog made me believe she WAS better than me!

I got home and I told my mom what happened. She could barely understand me because I couldn't stop crying.

My mom told me to go up to my room and lie down. She said she would call and let her mom know I couldn't go to the movies today.

In my room, I couldn't stop sobbing! I was thinking about how I've wanted a dog so bad for years, and how I would be so happy and grateful to have one.

And she just treats it like it's nothing and rubs it in my face, because she knows that I've always wanted a dog!

My mom came up to talk to me after she called to tell them I couldn't go and said, "Chloe, Samantha getting a dog will be a great thing. When you get your dog she will have an instant playmate. I think when you get some rest you will feel better about the whole thing."

I got to thinking...I did get up earlier than normal. Maybe I am tired and over emotional. I got back in bed and closed my eyes.

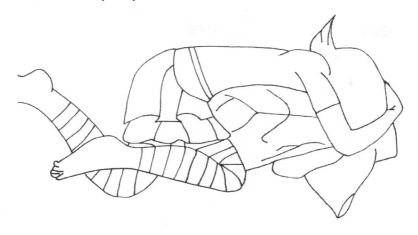

When I woke up, I did some more thinking about what my mom said about my dog having an instant playmate, and I think my mom is right.

I had not thought about my dog needing a doggie friend to go on walks with.

I am just so ready to have my OWN new dog, NOW!!!

June 5

So today I went over to the course to play golf by myself, because we have a tournament coming up and I needed to work on a few things.

Sometimes it is so enjoyable to play by myself.

Today I was really enjoying being alone because it was nice weather...not too hot, and there was a nice breeze.

It was really a great time to think and work on the weaknesses in my game.

I finished playing the first hole, and as I was teeing off on the #2 tee box, I look back and Scott was just finishing on the green of #1 (which is right by the #2 tee box).

He was playing by himself and I am by myself.

As soon as I finished hitting my tee shot on #2 he walks over to the tee box.

I didn't want to be rude so I asked him if he wanted to join me, and he said, "Sure."

Scott is one of Tyler's good friends, and he is also a pretty good golfer. He seems nice and is cute too.

I think to myself...this will be fine, it shouldn't be too bad.

We finished #2, teed off on #3, and we were walking and talking in the fairway between shots.

He really is a nice guy.

He is 14, the same age as Tyler, and he was Mackenzie's partner in the last youth scramble we played in. He is fun to talk to and seems to be easy going; I see why him and Tyler are good friends.

We were walking up to the #4 green
and our bags clanked together and
something on them got hung.

Scott put his hand on my shoulder to
stabilize us so we didn't fall, and we
started laughing and trying to pull
them apart.

He then wraps his arm around my
shoulder so we can move our bags
closer together to unhook them.

As soon as I look up, there is Mackenzie and her Mom, about 20 feet away from us in their golf cart.

I start to wave and say something to them, but the next thing I know Mackenzie pulls out her phone, takes a picture of us, and they drive off.

As they are driving off I shouted at
them, "Hey...Mackenzie...what are you
doing?"

She and her mom never answered as
they were heading toward the
clubhouse.

About that time our bags came unhooked and we walked up to the green to putt.

I now have nine million things running through my head!

Why did she do that?
Why wouldn't she answer me?
What is the picture for?
What is wrong with her?

I am so upset and becoming furious.

So much so that I can't even concentrate!

I am so distracted I end up 3 putting the green.

Then I hit a terrible tee shot on #5.

I could NOT pull myself together!

I told myself I NEED to pull it together...if for nothing else to act like nothing is bothering me in front of Scott!

He is going to think I am so weird!

In my head, it finally hits me…she is going to send that picture to Tyler. She is going to make it look like something it is not!

Now I AM SO MAD!!!!! I can't focus!

I decide that when I finish 9 holes, I am heading in the clubhouse to look for her!

I am going to confront her and ask her why she took the picture, and what she needs it for.

Now that I have my plan in place I calm down some…enough to hit the ball at least.

I was trying to be nice to Scott and not act upset because it was not his fault. But, I don't think that I hid my feelings very well.

As soon as we finish 9, I tell him I am hungry and am going to head in and get something to eat. I told him I had fun playing with him and I would catch him later.

He was so nice! He replied, "No problem. I enjoyed playing with you too today. We will have to do it again sometime." I said, "Yeah, it was fun! Absolutely!"

I could not get in the clubhouse fast enough!

I was going to find Mackenzie and ask her WHY she took that picture of us, and WHAT was she going to use it for?

I mean it wasn't like she was even sneaky about it…she drove straight up to us and snapped it! With her mom in the cart, too!

I looked everywhere around the club and couldn't seem to find her, but I am not leaving UNTIL I find her!

I sit at a table and get some water to drink, and here she comes bee-bopping around the corner all smiles!

I say loudly and firmly, "Hey, Mackenzie! Why did you take that picture of me and Scott on hole #4?"

She says with a smirk on her face, "Wh- What?? Ummmm...what are you talking about?"

I could tell she was nervous!

I said in a forceful voice, "MACKENZIE, YOU CAME UP TO ME, PRACTICALLY RIGHT IN MY FACE, AND SNAPPED A PICTURE WITH YOUR PHONE!"

She said, "Oh, um, my mom and I wanted a picture of what good shape the fairways are in to send to a friend."

I am dumbfounded! I don't even know what to say. I just paused, and looked at her with my forehead wrinkled up.

But I am thinking...REALLY, of all the fairways, she needed a picture of the one we were walking on.

I didn't want to fight with her!
I decided to let it go for now and come up with a different plan after I have time to think and calm down.

She bounced on up the stairs at the
clubhouse with a big smile on her face
and said, "Catch you later, Chloe."

June 6

Anytime our coach teaches us something new, it never feels right the first few times I try it.

Today our coach, who is an amazing coach, was working with us around the green.

My mom happened to be the one who took us to our lesson today. I love my mom, but she can be so annoying!!

When she goes to our golf lessons she takes a chair and sits and listens to everything our golf coach tells us.

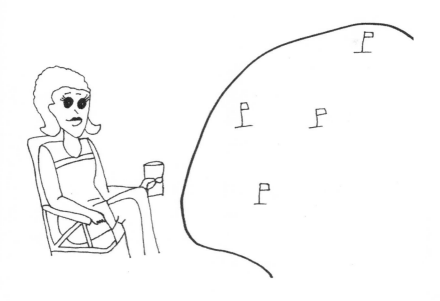

She says she learns a lot by just listening to his tips.

So today our coach was working with us on our shots from the apron of the green.

The apron is the area that is just around the green that is closely cut.

My brother uses his sand wedge for almost everything around the green.

Our coach told Caleb he used to do that when he was playing on the tour, but he got tired of losing!

He said he paid $5000 to go to a clinic to help him improve his short game, and he learned this one tip that would help him chip the ball within 5 feet of the cup almost every time.

The tip is, when you are on the apron of the green, you take an iron and angle your body toward the hole, put your weight on your front foot, ball placement on the back foot and use a putting stroke and let the ball run to the hole. Depending on how far you are from the hole will determine your club choice and how far the ball will roll.

So he demonstrates this tip for us.

My mom is all ears and soaking up every word!!!!

All
Ears

Listening
all the time!

After our lesson today we went out as a family and played 9 holes.

My mom took what she heard from today's lesson and tried it for herself.

The only problem is my mom is sometimes too vocal and a little dramatic!!!

Every time she thought WE should be using the new technique from today... and we didn't...she would let us know.

And, when SHE used the tip and chipped it closer to the hole than Caleb or I, I would hear her say, "I am terrible at chipping and I chipped it closer than both of you...$5000 tip, baby!"

IT IS SO ANNOYING!!!!

She said she really believes in it because it has helped her so much and BLAH BLAH BLAH!!

Caleb and I look at each other, I roll my eyes, and we move on to the next hole.

The next hole she has another shot from the apron of the green.

We both know it is coming and are ready for her display of the $5000 tip!!!

Caleb and I look at each other and just wait, because we know what is coming.

Before she hits the shot she calls out, "$5000 tip being used right here!"

She takes the club back, makes her stroke and we watch the ball roll...AND SHE CHIPS IT IN THE CUP!

$5000 tip baby!

In the hole

She raises her hands in the air and says, "It WORKS!!" Like she is rubbing it in our faces.

She says, "I love a bargain! That right there is a $5000 bargain! I am the worst one, and now I can chip it in! You two should be using it!"

Caleb and I both have honestly had enough!

We look at each other, we try to be mad, but we start laughing because we cannot believe it! She is the worst golfer in our family and she is doing awesome with this tip!

She goes on and on about how amazing our coach is. She loves his tips, and we need to make sure we are using it.

She is still talking...and goes on to say if we are in position to use the shot and we choose not to we are throwing away $5000!!!

It really gets exhausting!

I understand her point. After watching her I know we need to use it, but that doesn't make her any less annoying at the moment!!

June 7

My Mom's and Dad's favorite golfer of all time is Byron Nelson.

Byron Nelson

They always use him as an example for Caleb and me, and they read to us from his books to help us with our golf game.

Byron won 11 straight PGA golf tournaments, 11 weeks in a row, in 1945.

He is no longer alive, but he was a great golfer.

He was also an amazing example of how a true gentleman behaves and was a wonderful Christian man.

We have many of his books at our house. My mom will reference parts from his books when she is talking to us about golf, and she uses his words and stories to inspire us.

Caleb and I played in a 9-hole tournament today and we both won our age group.

When you win your age group in the 9-hole tournaments you get to pick out a flag.

They come in all different colors.

Caleb picked out a red one today and I picked out a pink one...OF COURSE!!!

On the way home Caleb was looking out the window and said, "I am happy we both won."

He continued looking out the window but was quiet for a while.

Then he asked my mom a question.

He said, "Mom, do you think I could win 11 straight golf tournaments?"

My mom quickly replied, "I don't know Caleb, that is really hard to do!"

She continued with, "There are some amazing players on tour today that don't even come close and" Caleb interrupted and said, "MOM! Not on the PGA tour, on the local junior tour."

My mom replied, "OHHHH, if you work hard you sure can."

I saw my mom and dad look at each other and smile.

Caleb then replied, "Well, this is two weeks in a row. Just 9 more to go!"

When we got home Caleb was feeling pumped.

He found his flag from last week and took the one from today and hung them both in his room on the wall and said he is going to fill his wall up with them.

CALEB'S ROOM

He walked down the hall to the
bathroom after hanging his flags on
the wall and said, "Instead of taking a
shower tonight I believe I will be
taking a victory bath!"

VICTORY BATH

I got to thinking about how excited Caleb is for his wins and was thinking about myself.

I have won 2 weeks =in a row as well.

I know winning every week is really hard at any level in golf!
Especially on the Ladies Professional Golf Association (LPGA) and Professional Golf Association (PGA) tours. These are the tours for the highest level of golf.

On tour it is hard to win even two weeks in a row.

I decided, for fun, to add another element to Caleb's goal.

I am going to see if Caleb wants to have a competition with me and we will see who can be the first person to win 11 tournaments, but they don't have to be in a row.

That way if one person doesn't win one week, the competition is not over.

I really enjoy playing in both 9 and 18 hole tournaments.

I am glad we can pick to play in both.

I decide to also hang my flags on my wall in my room. It really is fun to win!

CHLOE'S ROOM

June 8

So I am learning that golf can be like a roller coaster.

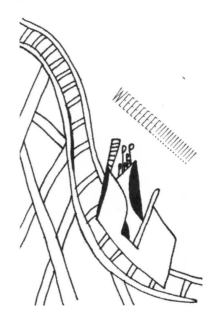

WEEEEEEEEE!!!!!!!!!!

One day you are doing great, swinging the club well, and putting well.

The next day you can feel like you
have never picked up a golf club a day
in your life!

I don't get it!

But it does help keep me humble, never full of myself, and it ALWAYS keeps me practicing hard.

It also helps me understand boys a little better, because golf can be so unpredictable...JUST LIKE BOYS!

Having a brother kind of helps me understand boys...sometimes...but most days, I never know if a boy at the golf course is going to be nice or moody!

Today when I went over to the putting green, Scott was on the putting green with his ear buds in. I smiled and waved to him.

He looked straight at me with a blank look and kept putting.

I understand trying to focus and work on your game, but acting like you don't even know me is just weird.

I mean we are the only two on the putting green, which isn't all that big. And, we just played 9 holes together 2 days ago!

When we played together he acted like he had a good time hanging out and talking.

He seemed nice at the time, but he was hitting the ball pretty good that day.

After he left the putting green, I saw him walk over to the range and hit balls...and he wasn't hitting them very well at all!!

I am wondering if boys are nice when they are hitting the ball well and rude when they are not.

It is ridiculous for me to have to know how they are hitting the ball before talking to them.

I mean, as far as I can tell...Tyler seems to always be nice to me.
But to me, Tyler IS a little better golfer than Scott.

But, when I played with Scott the other day he seemed so nice.

I don't get it, because today I am seeing a whole other side to Scott!

I wonder if it is because Tyler has Tessa, who is my age, and maybe having a sister helps him understands girls better.

I know having a brother helps me understand boys a little better.

Who knows! I just know that I like people to be the same every time I see them!

My papa says that you should always pay attention to people when they are playing sports because it will reveal a lot about their true personality.

Maybe I am getting to see that Scott is truly moody!

I will make a mental note for future reference!

I keep practicing on my putting and Scott is over on the range.

Next thing I know I see him take his iron, raise it over his head, and tomahawk it on the ground over and over.

I stopped putting and was staring at him with my mouth open.

I wanted to laugh but I didn't, because if he looked over and saw me he would be so mad at me!

I know it is no fun to hit bad shots, but how you handle it is a mark of how mature you are.

I just don't understand throwing and slamming clubs.

Sure I get upset when I am not doing well, but ultimately...it is just a game!!

When I get upset I always remind myself that some people are going hungry, some people can't see, or hear, or walk.

My papa, who is a counselor, taught me this technique. He said it is called reframing. Reframing means to think about your feelings in a different way.

He said when you get upset take a deep breath. Count to 3 and reframe your anger with thankfulness.

I have done this and it really does help.

I don't think now is the time to share this tip with Scott, but he needs to learn how to reframe things!

June 9

SQUEEEEEEEEEEEEE!!!!!!!!!

I have been soooo excited this morning!

Every since I opened my eyes I have been thinking about how today is the day I get to go to the Paw Pal's shelter with TYLER!!!

DOUBLE SQUEEEEEEEE!!!!!!!!!!

There is nothing better than my GBF (I think???) and PUPPIES!!!!

Tyler offered to pick me up on his way, but my mom said she was going

to be out running errands and it would
be easier for her to drop me off.

It is 4:00 and I am right on time
arriving at the Paw Pal's Animal
Shelter.

As soon as we pull in, Tyler is waiting
at the door to greet me.

We walked in, he introduced me to the owners, and then he took me on a tour around the facility.

We started in the small dog section.

As we went to each cage, Tyler took the puppy out and handed it to me.

I played with the puppy while Tyler cleaned the cage and got fresh food and water for each one.

I took my cell phone out to take selfies of me with each dog.

That way, when I got home, I could go through my pictures of each one that is available.

Tyler said, "Chloe, let me have your phone. I will take a picture of you with each one, that way when you get home you can show them to your parents."

I squealed and told him, "That is a great idea!"

I handed my phone to Tyler and he took pictures, along with some video of me playing with each dog.

After we got to the third puppy I was realizing I LOVE ALL THE PUPPIES!

They were all so cute and sweet, and I would love to have any one of these puppies and give them a good home!

We moved on to the fourth cage and there was a small black and white puppy inside.

I couldn't make it out until Tyler reached in and handed it to me.

IT WAS A BABY BOSTON TERRIER!!!

I squealed in a high pitch and jumped up and down with my arms flailing.

This is the type of dog that all my research says will be the perfect dog for our family.

I told Tyler, "I HAVE TO HAVE THIS PUPPY!"

I quickly asked him, "Why is this dog in an animal shelter? It is just a baby puppy."

He said he would go find out.

He came back and said, "She was brought in by an elderly lady. She said her family from out of town bought her a puppy and after a couple of weeks she realized it had too much energy for her so she wasn't able to keep her."

I told Tyler AGAIN, "I HAVE TO HAVE THIS PUPPY!!"

Looking at this sweet little puppy I couldn't wipe the smile off my face!

I tried to call my parents but they didn't pick up. I was dying!

I told Tyler, "I don't want anyone else to get this puppy! Can we hide her?"

He laughed and said, "I don't think so, but I will check with the owners of the shelter and see what can be done."

I didn't want to move on to the next cage. I was afraid to put this sweet little puppy down.

Tyler snapped a few more pictures of me with her and said we have to move on because we have 4 more cages to clean.

He said he would keep an eye on her to make sure no one got her until I can talk to my parents.

It was so hard for me to leave her, but I had to trust that Tyler would help me to get this cute, perfect for me, little puppy!

When we finished cleaning all the cages, we went up to talk to the owners about the little Boston puppy.

They said the vet had not checked her out yet.

They said the Veterinarian comes every Tuesday and checks out the new dogs they have received.

The dogs are not available for adoption until they have had a veterinarian check up.

Okay, I relaxed a little knowing that I had until Tuesday and that no one else could get my puppy.

June 10

I cannot stop looking at the pictures on my phone of my little Baby Boston and I am reading constantly about Boston Terriers on the Internet.

BOSTON TERRIERS ARE SO CUTE!

OH MY GOODNESS!

SHE IS PERFECT!

Everything I read about them sounds perfect...well...except for one thing.

It says they have really bad gas and
fart all the time.

PHEW!!!!

I am going to leave this part out when
selling the idea of this puppy to my
family!

To help me stop obsessing over my
puppy I head over to the driving range
to hit balls.

As I am approaching the range I see
Mackenzie.

She waves at me and seems to be acting totally normal.

HEY CHLOE

I walk up to her and say, "Hey, Mackenzie".

I set up my bag beside her and start to stretch to warm up before I hit balls.

We are chitchatting back and forth about nothing important.

In my head I am thinking...I like her, I want to trust her, but I don't trust her! I want to, but I just can't!

I think her competitiveness makes her do weird things...like taking that picture of Scott and me.

I cannot stop thinking about what she might be doing with that picture!!

Thankfully, I have a backup plan in place to find out.

I told Tessa the whole story, just in case Mackenzie tried to send the picture to Tyler and make it seem like something it isn't.

Tessa told me she would let me know if Tyler got a text from Mackenzie with a picture attached.

So, I have totally put it out of my mind...at least I have tried too!

As I am swinging my 5-iron I hear my phone ding...I got a text.

I walk over to look at it and see it is from Tessa and it says:
Mackenzie sent a picture to Tyler.

The minute I read that my heart dropped.

WHY ? ? WHAT ?
? ?

How do I act normal
after reading this?

I can't even look at Mackenzie!! I feel sick!!

My first thought is WHEN DID SHE SEND IT?? She is right beside me.

Then I realize Tessa probably just found out, but it probably wasn't sent just now.

I am standing right next to Mackenzie, trying to act normal, but I don't hide my emotions very well.

I decide to start swinging my 5-iron again so I can hide my face from her.

I am standing over the ball and can barely concentrate.

All these thoughts are going through my head:

WHAT IS WRONG WITH HER!!
WHY DOES SHE TRY TO RUIN MY LIFE!!
I AM SO MAD I WANT TO SCREAM!!!!!
SHOULD I CONFRONT HER NOW???!!!
I am wrestling with confronting her NOW!!!

I am so torn because I want to be friends with Mackenzie, but she makes it almost impossible.

You must have trust in a friendship and I don't trust her!!!

I do some thinking while I am hitting my 5-iron.

I decide to walk over to respond to Tessa's text, but I act like I am getting a drink of water and checking the time on my phone.

I texted Tessa back and I ask her... What is it a picture of?

She responded and said:
I don't know but I will try to find out.

I have a sick feeling in my stomach.

I want to confront Mackenzie NOW, but I decide to take a deep breath and try to act normal until I find out exactly WHAT picture Mackenzie texted Tyler.

UGGGGG!!!!!

THIS IS SOOOOOO HARD!!!!!

June 11

One thing that is coming up in almost every golf tournament I play is a girl telling me a score that is different than what I counted for her.

I don't know if it is on purpose, or if they are used to their parents keeping their score...whatever the reason it happened again today.

I mean...it could just be an accident.

I know I am not perfect and have said the wrong score before as well.

Once I said a score too high and once a score too low.

So I get it...no one is perfect!!

But when I have this happen...I want to know what to do.

So I asked my dad.

 He told me a polite way to handle someone giving you the wrong score is to kindly say, "Oh, I had a 6 for you (or whatever that score was).

Give them a chance to think about it and respond. If they disagree with you go through the strokes with them. And most importantly, you never start the next hole until you are both in agreement."

When I was playing my match today, the girl I was playing with told me a score lower than what I counted for her.

Even though I was uncomfortable asking her to count it out, I knew I needed to work on this.

So I gently said, "Julie, I had a 6 for you."

She paused, thought about it, looked at her dad. They counted the strokes out together and she said, "Oh, yeah. It was a 6."

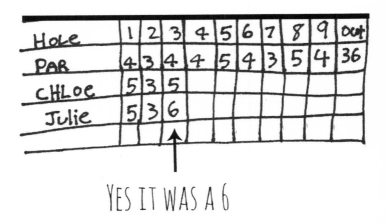

Hole	1	2	3	4	5	6	7	8	9	out
Par	4	3	4	4	5	4	3	5	4	36
Chloe	5	3	5							
Julie	5	3	6							

YES IT WAS A 6

I am so proud of myself. I don't like to confront ever!!!

I was nice about it. She was nice about it.

Golf helps with so many other life skills as well as being a fun sport!!

I don't think her mistake was intentional, but she told me she got a 5 when I counted a 6.

And I was sure she had a 6. I remembered all the strokes.

It felt awkward and empowering at the same time. Awkward confronting her but empowering because I stood up to what I felt was not correct.

I usually would just let it go and tell my parents about it when I got home.

My dad always tells me it is my responsibility to handle it, and today I did.

I am so proud of myself!

June 12

I LOVE me some RICKIE FOWLER!!!!

My dad...not so much!

But...I found out the most amazing information about MY RICKIE.

I know once I share this with my dad he will also have a great reason to LOVE him some RICKIE!!!

My dad, he always makes fun of me for loving Rickie.

I cheer for him...loudly...when I see him on the TV.

I am always reading about him online.

Watching YouTube videos about him or watching his social media updates.

I DO NOT understand what my dad's problem is. RICKIE IS the BEST!!! RICKIE IS AMAZING!!!!!

I have a great plan that will fix my dad.

One of the reasons my dad likes Byron Nelson so much, and uses him as a role model for us, is because he was a great Christian man with high morals.

Well I found out today that SO. IS. MY. RICKIE!!

I read online that he doesn't drink
AND goes to bible study regularly.

They have a bible study on tour that
several of the players attend like
Bubba Watson, Ben Crane, Zach
Johnson and...MY RICKIE!

I read that My RICKIE will put bible
verses on his ball markers. He did this
in the Ryder Cup one year and birdied
the last 4 holes on Sunday.

When I tell my dad about this he will have to LOVE him!!!

So tonight, I am sitting at the kitchen table while my mom is finishing cooking our dinner. I can't wait to give my dad the good news.

We all sit down. My dad says the blessing for the food.

When he finished I think, now is the perfect time to tell my dad about MY RICKIE.

So I start, "Dad, I have the best news for you!" He replies, "Okay."

"Dad, did you know that MYYYYYY RICKIE does not drink alcohol and goes to the weekly bible study on the tour."

I say this with such pride and am ready for my dad to burst out with the words that he agrees with me that RICKIE IS AMAZING!!

He should totally agree with me because RICKIE IS the most amazing and wonderful golfer and person.

I mean...HOW COULD HE NOT!!!

He finishes chewing his food and slowly replies, "I am glad he does go to bible study. I want everyone to love and know God."

I am just looking at him.
Dumbfounded. How come he didn't say
RICKIE IS AMAZING?

I mean, his response is good, but I
wanted him to say RICKIE IS THE
BEST EVER!!!! AND FEEL LIKE I DO!!!

I guess he will still tease me when it
comes to MY RICKIE, but at least he
knows I like a good person!!

June 13

Today, I have an 18-hole golf tournament and I am so excited!

My dad is out of town, so my Pops came along and is going to be my caddy. My mom is going to caddy for Caleb. :)

I love when my Pops caddies for me. He is so supportive and so much fun to play with!

The only issue with today's tournament is...my brother tees off an hour and a half before me.

So, I will have to hang out for extra time because we get to the course an hour before his tee time.

This puts me there 2 1/2 hours before my tee time.

I don't mind it most of the time… but today it is sooooo HOT, and the heat will make the wait feel so much longer!!

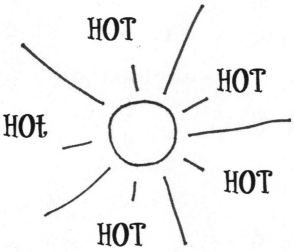

I decide to go ahead and warm up
with Caleb.

We went over and hit balls on the
range and then went and practiced
putting and chipping.

I knew I had a while before my tee
time, but I figured I'd go ahead and
warm up with him because I had
nothing else to do.

When Caleb went to tee off, I had around an hour or so before my tee time.

On this course the first hole went out and the second hole came back.

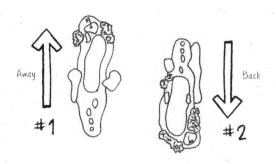

So my pops and I figured we would follow along with Caleb and watch him play the first two holes because it would bring us back to the #1 tee box, and I was already warmed up.

Caleb didn't play the first or second hole well.

He sometimes gets too excited on the first few holes and plays too fast.

He hit his tee shot on #1 pretty good, but he duffed his second shot and ended up making a double bogey.

A Double Bogey is when the golfer makes a score of 2-over the par on an individual golf hole.

Then on hole #2 he hit a good drive, but it went a little right and was close to a fence.

Caleb's ball

My mom was trying to decide if he could get relief from the fence with no penalty.

She asked the dad who was caddying for the boy playing with Caleb and he said he didn't know.

Caleb could still make an okay swing at it so he decided not to risk getting a penalty stroke added.

He could have played two balls and gotten a ruling when he finished to know which score to count. You must get the ruling before you sign your scorecard.

We did find out later that he would have had to play the ball as it was because the unplayable ruling is:

The player may deem his ball unplayable at any place on the course, except when the ball is in a water hazard. The player is the sole judge as to whether his ball is unplayable. But if a ball is unplayable then he adds a one-stroke penalty.

Caleb ended up with a double bogey on the second hole.

My mom was so frustrated with him because Caleb wouldn't slow down or listen to anything she was telling him.

Caleb doesn't truly listen to anything anyone tells him!!! He is hard headed and always does things his way!!

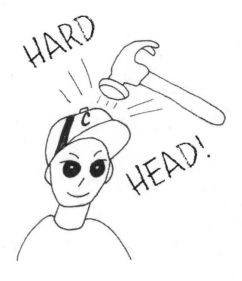

Finally my mom decided it would be best today to send my pops with Caleb and she'd go with me.

My pops agreed, and after two more holes, he texted my mom and said Caleb birdied hole #3 and parred #4.

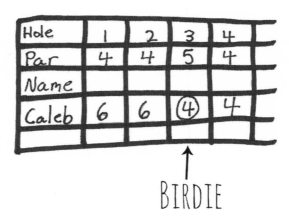

Hole	1	2	3	4
Par	4	4	5	4
Name				
Caleb	6	6	④	4

BIRDIE

Pops is so fun to play with because he is so relaxed and let's you do your own thing.

Which is just what Caleb is going to do anyway.

So I was still waiting...and waiting...and finally, it had come time for me to tee off; I was more than warmed up.

Only thing is, I didn't eat while I was waiting...not realizing that I had been there almost 3 hours before I teed off.

I played with two other girls today, one who is super slow and the other is a total Brat.

I usually get paired with really nice girls, but not today!

I already knew their reputations and it wasn't for good reasons!

On the first hole, I hit an okay drive; it got a good bounce, which helped.

The other two girls hit it okay, but it didn't turn out great.

I hit a good second shot and they both duffed theirs, one which went into the water.

I was feeling pretty good and played the first 9 holes really well.

But, unfortunately as good of a start as I had...I had an equally rough back 9.

I really felt tired and done by the time we finished 9 holes. Play was slow and it took us 2 and a half hours to finish the front 9.

I was hungry, thirsty, and ready to quit!

Putting 2 and 2 together...I realized I had already been at the course for 5 hours by the time we finished 9.

9 holes in 5 hours =

I AM D.O.N.E

Just as we turned to head to the back 9 it started raining, and they blew a horn, which signaled for us to come in.

I was thinking, YES, we are done!!!

I AM SO TIRED AND HUNGRY!
But then they came and told us to hang around and to wait and see if the storm passes.

We waited and waited, and then an hour and a half later they sent us back out.

By this time...I have been at the course for almost 7 hours and still have another 9 holes to play.

7 hours AND still 9 holes left

Every fiber in my body was REBELLING going back on that golf course.

I was HUNGRY, HOT, and THIRSTY, and I was DONE!!

My mom kept trying to get me to eat and drink, but I wasn't having it.

I didn't even feel like I was in my own skin anymore!

I was so tired that I couldn't be reasoned with.

On the 10th hole, when we went back out, I played horrible!

I hit a drive into the water and had to take a penalty.

The water where I hit my ball was marked with a red stake, so I have the lateral hazard option. So I dropped the ball within two club-lengths of the point where the ball last crossed into the water.

I knew the reason I was taking a penalty was because I lost concentration and I was feeling miserable!!

I knew I wasn't nourishing myself at all, but I couldn't think logically anymore, and I just wanted to quit!!

As I think back now I try to figure out why I wouldn't eat or drink something. I know I kept thinking...I don't want to get weighed down and I want to focus.

Unfortunately, that rationale was getting me nowhere!

Honestly, I needed some food and water.

I was really beyond thinking straight!

CAN'T THINK!!

HUNGRY!!

BRATS!!

HOT!!

DONE!!

THIRSTY!!

In the moment, I didn't know what was wrong with me, and I didn't know how to fix it.

Thinking back now, I get it...but at the time, I was out of my head! BEYOND LOGICAL!

Then add one brat and one slow player to the mix and I was over this whole day!!!

With 3 holes left to play I stopped talking to my mom, or anyone for that matter.

I was swinging the club, but I no longer felt I was even in my own body.

My stomach was cramping and it felt like someone was taking my organs and twisting them inside me.

ALL my circumstances were not good!!

I had a flashback to when I was figure skating. I would do this same thing...I wouldn't eat the whole day of a competition, and I would feel sick and have headaches.

In skating, it was my nerves as to why I wouldn't eat. I don't know what my problem was today, because it was not nerves.

I think it was poor planning and poor preparation on my part.

I got there 2 and a half hours early, didn't hydrate or nourish myself properly. Now add the slow player and the brat, the rain delay, the heat and wet grass, it was all too much for me to handle!

At this point, I was so illogical I started to wonder if golf was even the sport for me.

I ended up placing 2nd in this tournament, but it was not about placement at all for me today!

I know I didn't manage myself well, which caused me to not do my best.

The physical pain I was feeling was also a lesson to me on how important it is to manage my food, hydrate properly on the golf course, and keep my sugar levels up.

It turned out I was there a total of 9 hours...with getting there early, playing a slow round, and dealing with a rain delay.

9 hours = me out of my head!

By the end of the day I was so over the day, and I knew there has to be a better way!!

As I think back to when we had the rain delay, I remembered seeing the 2 girls I was playing with both eating sandwiches.

My mom had packed me a sandwich. I don't know why I didn't do the same...I guess inexperience on my part.

I know I see the pros on TV eat and drink all the time in a round, and it makes sense because golf matches take several hours!

Even though I didn't do my best today I still learned so much!

From now on, I know I need a strategy for keeping myself nourished and hydrated.

It can be so overwhelming when you think of all the things you must do in a round of golf.

Trying to focus on playing well, feeling well, staying hydrated, not getting too hot.

Golf is about WAY MORE than just how you hit the ball.

June 14

Today is TUESDAY!

SQUEEEEEEE!!!!!!!

All I want to do is go get my doggie at Paw Pals! I can't wait to bring her home and take her to play golf with me!

I hope the veterinarian checks her out first thing today so she will be ready for us when we get there.

I went downstairs for breakfast and asked my mom what time we were going to the shelter today.

She replied, "Honey, I am so sorry, but your Grandma is sick and we are going to go over and help her today."

I wanted to scream! NOOOOOOOO THIS CAN'T BE HAPPENING!!!!!!!

I love my Grandma, and I want to help her, but why can't we do BOTH???!!!

I don't want ANYONE to get MY PUPPY!

My mom told me we would try to stop by on the way home from my grandparents' house if we had time.

As I am helping my Grandma that morning I could not get my mind off of my puppy.

I worked so hard and fast to MAKE SURE we would have enough time to go by and get her.

Thankfully we did finish in time, so we could stop by the shelter about an hour before it closed, which should be plenty of time for us to visit, hold her, and fill out paperwork so we can bring her home.

We pulled in the parking lot and there was a CLOSED sign across the front door with some orange tape.

WHAT!!!! WHY!!!!!!!!!

I was freaking out!!! Trying not to cry, I took a picture of the front entrance and texted it to Tyler and said, "The dog shelter says CLOSED. What happened??"

He said he had just found out a few minutes ago himself, and he couldn't believe it either!

He said he just got a text from the owner, and he said they ran out of money.

The shelter runs off of donations, and they had fallen 2 months behind on the rent.

I asked Tyler if there was any way I could still get my little Boston baby puppy.

He said he would find out what he could and he would call me later.
I can't believe this!

This is what I was afraid of. My chances of getting my puppy are being yanked right out from under me.

I feel like I can't breathe. My hands are shaking, and I can't even feel my face anymore.

My mom told me to calm down and take deep breaths! We would do what we could.

I just couldn't help it; tears are rolling down my face.

I was SURE, from the moment I saw the little puppy at the shelter, that she was MY little puppy.

I am just heartbroken!

June 17

I have been so upset about the shelter closing that I haven't written in my journal for 2 days.

I decided to keep my mind off of my little puppy by pouring myself into my golf game.

After my last tournament I am on a mission to find a better hydration and nourishment plan!

My mom said she was going to help me find solutions, because my last tournament was an experience we don't want to repeat.

She is watching TV with my dad, and she called me into the living room and put the TV on pause.

She said, "Here is your Rickie in a tournament eating and hydrating while playing."

My mom knew if there was one way to get me to want to solve a problem quickly, it was to have me want to do what MY RICKIE does.

Seeing him didn't get me thinking about nutrition but thinking about him!

I decided to Google about "My Rickie" and I did see some nutritional things he adheres to.

He said he tries to always eat..."Trainer Approved" snacks.

Rickie said he usually goes for the fruit because it is "Trainer Approved".

My mom suggested I also talk to some of the competitive ladies at our club and get ideas for what they use for snacks and food during their rounds.

I think I will because I can't feel like I did in my last tournament ever again!

June 19

I have been noticing when I play tournaments that all the better golfers have their name embroidered on the zipper pouch of their golf bag.

I played with the same girl a few weeks ago that I am playing with today.

A few weeks ago she didn't have a bag with her name on it, but today she showed up with a new bag that had her name on it.

Not only did it have her name on it but it had #GOMO embroidered below her name.

While we were walking I asked her what #GOMO meant, and she said it stood for "Go Mo Martin."

She said Melissa "Mo" Martin is her favorite player on the LPGA tour, and she has been following her for years.

She said Mo won the Women's British Open in 2014, but she had been following her for several years even before she won.

She said she would follow her at local golf events and MO would always talk to her while she played and she was always so nice.

She said at one of the events she was going to follow her at, she sent her a good luck message on social media before her tournament.

MO responded to her and asked her if she would come and go to dinner with her after her first round.

She said it was so cool, and they talked about all kinds of fun stuff.

It made me wish I had a relationship with my favorite player on the LPGA tour.

I have so many I love, but Lexi Thompson is my favorite.

I know the top players have so many obligations.

I decided I am going to find a favorite player to follow who is outside the top 20 on tour.

I want to look for one that I have a lot in common with.

I would love to learn more about ALL the different touring pros.

So I went on the Internet and printed off a list of the top 100 female golfers on the LPGA.

I then made a chart with each of the players names and what their interests were.

Pets

Fashion

Beliefs

Practice Habits

Hobbies

Age started playing

I studied their styles, beliefs, values, swings, animals, foods they liked, and things they loved outside of golf.

I wanted to find the player that I have the most in common with.

I was having so much fun reading about all these ladies. So many of their stories were so interesting!

Because there were so many awesome stories, I quickly realized this project was going to take me longer than a day.

I decide to set it aside and come back to it once the summer is over, because I will have more time when I am not playing tournaments every weekend.

One of the things I love about playing in individual events is when I play with someone nice, you have 4 hours to walk and talk, and they usually share some of the cool things they have done or are doing.

I loved hearing about Mo Martin today.

When I got home I read up on her, and now I will always look for her name and follow her in tournaments.

June 20

So I see I have a text from Tessa.

I am so scared to look at it because I have been waiting for her to find out what picture Mackenzie sent to Tyler's cell phone.

I am not sure how I am going to react if it is the one of Scott and I!!!

Before I read Tessa's text, I first take a deep breath so my head doesn't explode!!

I read the text and it is just as I thought...

Tessa said, "Yes, it was a picture of you and Scott, but Mackenzie captioned the picture...the fairways look good."

The fairways look good

I am so mad I could scream.

Why would she do this to me...to us?

WHY???

Scott and Tyler are friends.

I thought Mackenzie and I were friends.

What is wrong with her???!!!

There's more than one fairway to take a picture of at PWCC!

If that is what she wanted to show him, why did she need to send one

with Scott and I in it and the fairway
in the BACKGROUND??

I thought she was my GFF?! My Golf
Friend Forever!! Now I am not so sure!

My mind starts racing.

She knew all along what her
intentions were and was totally trying
to cover herself.

Technically, she wasn't lying when she said she was taking the picture to show a friend what good shape the fairways were in, but she knew she was misleading me!

And, I don't think showing him the shape of the fairways was the intention of the picture!!

I texted Tessa back to find out what Tyler said about the text.

THANKFULLY she said, "He laughed." PHEW!!!

I feel slightly relieved, but I am still upset!

Tessa then said, "He knows why she was sending the picture. He is aware of all she is capable of. He has had many run-ins with her over the years at PWCC."

While I am relieved, my stomach still feels sick from this news.

Tyler not being upset is a relief, but...I am sick that Mackenzie would do this!

She's always angling so hard for him to like her, and for him to NOT like me.

She doesn't even care if she makes me look bad.

I really would like to be her friend, but she makes it nearly impossible sometimes!!

I want to say something to her but I don't think it would do any good.

When I asked her why she took the picture, she knew she was misleading me when she said, "To send to a friend about the fairways at PWCC."

Her intentions weren't good! I don't know what I've done to make her so angry!

I am very disappointed in her!

She truthfully has no right to be going after me like this; doesn't she have better things to do than hurting her friends?

On the bright side, Tessa being Tyler's sister, she has let me know how Tyler feels about the picture and that gives me some relief.

I wonder if Mackenzie lies in bed at night and thinks of these things to do, or if her and her mom scheme up these ideas together? UGGGGGHHHH!!!!

June 21

So today, my mom and I ran into the PWCC ladies club champion on the putting green.

As mom was visiting with her, I walked over to say hello.

My mom said, "Chloe, you should ask her how to handle some of the struggles you had in the last tournament, and see if she has any advice for you."

I think this is a good idea. I mean, who would turn down advice from the ladies club champ?

GOOD IDEA! I COULD USE SOME TIPS!

I explained to her that I was getting so tired on the last few holes in my 18-hole tournaments. I told her I was not finishing well.

I told her that I actually took 2 triple bogies on the last few holes and I was too tired to even care.

I told her I was thinking that maybe my warm up was too early, because my brother always teed off an hour before me, so I was getting to the course two hours early.

She nodded her head as if she knew exactly what I was talking about.

She then told me she really focuses on keeping her blood sugar levels up throughout a match.

She said, "It can be just as important as your swing technique you work on."

She said she usually takes a sandwich and cuts in up into four squares and eats one square every few holes.

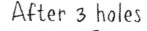
After 3 holes

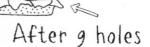

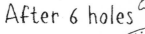
After 6 holes

After 9 holes

After 12 holes

She said she stays away from sugary drinks, but makes sure to drink lots of water, even if she doesn't think she is thirsty.

She also cuts up some fruit to pinch on every few holes.

She started to laugh and said she prepares an arsenal of food when she plays.

 **Sandwich**

 Fruit

She said when it is hot outside she learned a trick for the PB&J sandwich.

She said to put a thin coat of peanut butter on both sides of the sandwich and then the jelly in the middle. She said that way the jelly doesn't get the bread soggy.

All her ideas sound very helpful! I think I do get hungry, and hot, and mentally exhausted, and am beyond caring anymore.

I am going to really focus on managing my blood sugar and focusing on proper hydration and food and see if this helps me!

I told her, "Thank you so much for the advice! I think it will make a big difference for me."

She replied, "No problem, and oh, about getting there early. We used to face this often when I was in college. There was always some extra time for the girls with later tee times, so before the match they would hang out on the bus and only go warm up when it was one hour until tee off."

My mom chimed in and said, "Almost every course we play has a lounge of some kind. You could take a snack and

your phone and hang out indoors for a
bit."

I am so glad we talked to her.

Learning tips from her and hearing she
has faced some of the same struggles
I have can save me unnecessary pain
and STROKES!!!

Tyler texted me and said, "Me and Tessa are going to the range. See if you and Caleb can meet us there in an hour...I have a plan for Paw Pals!"

I asked my mom and texted him back, "She said yes, we will see you there."

We got over to the range and they were there hitting balls.

As soon as we walked up they stopped hitting, and we all four walked over and sat at one of the tables under the gazebo.

Tyler said he has been so hurt about
the shelter closing, but he has an
idea.

He said it is very last minute, but he
thought we could have a golf
tournament to raise funds this
weekend for the Paw Pals Animal
Shelter.

I immediately said "YES, I am in!"

Caleb said he was in too.

Tessa said, "I think we should get Mackenzie, Julie, and Kendal to help. We all ran a successful fundraiser before and I think the more people we have the better."

Even though I am not happy with Mackenzie right now, I decide to put aside all our differences for the sake of trying to save the shelter and get my little puppy.

So, I agreed with Tessa, because we do all make a great team.

Tessa said she was going to send a group text and see when we could all get together.

I told Tessa to get Tyler to text
Mackenzie...that way she will for sure
be there!

We both laughed and she said isn't
that the truth.

Tyler said he is going to text Scott
and some of the other junior boys to
see if they will join us.

We decide to have our meeting this
afternoon about the fundraising
tournament.

We know it is short notice but we have no time to waste if we are going to pull this together by the weekend.

Tyler said he was going to head out so he could organize the meeting material.

He gave Tessa his phone to send out texts to his junior golf friends.

Part of me wanted to look at his phone and see if he responded back to Mackenzie. But I didn't...I decided that I need to let it go. What's done is done!

We have a fundraiser tournament for Paw Pals we need to pull off, and I need to focus on that!

I am anxious and nervous! We just have to save the Paw Pals Animal Shelter.

There were 9 of us that showed up to the afternoon meeting: Tyler, Caleb, Tessa, Mackenzie, Julie, Stephanie, Scott, Adam, and Me.

Tyler starts the meeting by telling us he talked to the club and they said we COULD have an event this coming Saturday at 2:00.

He said they gave us 10 tee times for the event.

He said he thinks we should have 4 person teams and play captain's choice format.

A captain's choice format is where everyone tees off. The team selects the best drive. The rest of the golfers in the group simply pick up their golf ball and move up to the shot of choice. They place their ball within one club length of the best shot and they all hit again. You play this best ball format until the ball is in the cup. This format is great because it allows people who are not as good to still participate.

He thinks we will have the best tournament turnout if we focus on the members, because most of the members know a few of each of the junior players and will want to help us.

He said that he spoke with the owners of the Paw Pals shelter, and they are so excited and will be at the tournament to volunteer.

They have even offered to have puppies for adoption at the event and they will waive the adoption fee.

FREE CUTE PUPPIES FOR ADOPTION

Right now they have so many dogs to try and place in homes with the pending closing of the shelter.

Honestly, all I can think about is I have got to find my cute little doggie!

Tyler said he has played in many of these kinds of golf events before, and he has some good ideas for raising extra money for the shelter.

He said he thinks we should keep things simple due to our timeline:

1. Have an entry fee for the team and see if the club will let us keep half as a donation.

2. Sell mulligans for $5 and each person on the team can buy two.

3. On a par 5 we can have John, the head pro, hit a 300-yard tee shot for the team for $10.

4. Have longest drive and closest to the pin win a donated prize.

5. Have a raffle of some sort and get the club to help us with a prize.

We start trying to factor how much money we think we can make. The shelter has said they need $2000 to get all the bills paid to get back up and running.

We decide to assign jobs:

Scott says he will make a list of PWCC members who we know would probably play because they are always out on the course.

He said he would start making calls to see if we can get them to each put a team in.

He said he is also going to contact each of our parents and see if we can put any of them down for a team. This should give us a decent number of groups to start with.

I volunteered to run the raffle. I have a great idea for using my bunny Putt in a raffle.

Julie said she thinks we should also sell baked goods and have snack stands on holes 5 and 13.

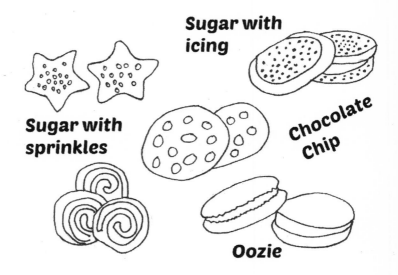

Sugar with icing

Sugar with sprinkles

Chocolate Chip

Oozie

I agree with her and tell her she would be perfect to run this because she did a great job last time baking for our fundraiser.

Julies baked cookies

Mackenzie said she would be in charge of selling mulligans.

Tessa said she will run the longest drive and Caleb can run closest to the pin.

I find it weird that Tessa is always pairing herself up with Caleb. She is older than he is, but they look the same age because they are the same height. I am just going to file this little piece of information away and watch those two!

We then start trying to factor how much money we think 10 teams will raise. We want to make sure we are able to reach our goal of $2000.

We decide to make the entry fee for each 4-person team $200.

We want to ask the club to donate half of the entry fee to the shelter.

If we can get 10 teams, the entry fee alone would put us halfway to our goal.

We then try to figure out the fees for longest drive, closest to pin, mulligans and raffle.

Tyler said he usually sees a mulligan sold for $5.

He said we can have the longest drive and closest to the pin on the front 9 included but have additional ones for $5 each on the back 9.

We start figuring out the money and how much profit we think each event will bring. We base our calculations on 10 teams entering.

Longest drive $250
Closest to pin $250
Entry fee $1000
Raffle $250
Mulligans $250
Total $2000

Just on these items alone we should be able to meet our goal of the $2000 needed to save the shelter.

We all have our assigned tasks and are so excited about the event this weekend.

June 25

I love hanging out with Tyler in the Clubhouse.

He tells the best stories.

He plays in more competitive tournaments, and some of his stories are crazy.

Today he was talking about a kid he played with a week ago. He said some of these boys act like they are pros on TV.

He said, "The tournament I played in last weekend allowed caddies. One kid I was paired with had a dad that had a bib on with their last name on it.

Every time his kid would hit the ball the dad would talk non-stop, saying things like, 'Great shot…That was amazing…You killed that one…Whoop whoop… That one is outta here.'"

As I am listening I was thinking how embarrassed I would be if my parents were doing that.

He said, "The kid played so slow! And if he was 60 yards from the green he would WALK up to the green and walk the perimeter of the green and then come back to his ball and take 4 practice swings."

I asked him, "What did you do? Did you say anything?"

Tyler said, "There is not much you can do. You can report it when you turn 9. But, if we get too far behind a person running the tournament will come give us a warning. But honestly, sometimes you just try to find ways to occupy yourself. While I was waiting, sometimes I would eat, get something to drink, look at my phone."

Slow pace of play is often determined by being at least one hole behind the group in front of you, but it can be based on criteria set by the tournament you are playing.

He also said, "Before the kid I was playing with would putt, EVERY TIME he would walk the perimeter of the green and then lay down to read the putt."

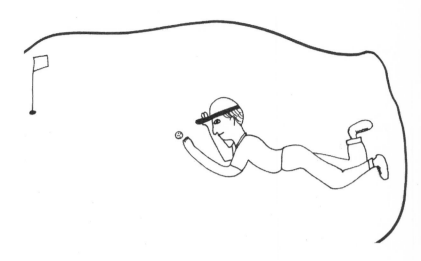

Caleb was listening and said, "Dude, how did you not laugh?"

Tyler said, "Well, in the heat I didn't think it was funny. I wanted him to hurry up! He also had his name on his golf balls. He lost one on the 12th hole and he started crying and shouted at me to help him find it."

I asked Tyler, "What did you do?"

Tyler said, "I was on the other side of the fairway. I just ignored him. I was trying to focus on my next shot and what I was going to do because my ball landed in a divot."

Caleb asked, "What do you do if your ball lands in the divot?"

He said, "You play it as it lies. But, you try to move the ball back in your stance a little and then take a normal swing."

The Divot ruling is that you can not move your ball out of a divot hole, even when the divot is in the fairway – if you do, you add a penalty stroke.

Tyler is so smart! I just love listening to him.

I don't know why but I giggle a lot when I am around him, and I can't stop smiling!

Even if what he is saying isn't funny...I still laugh.

I don't know what is wrong with me!

Sometimes I feel so weird about how I look when I am around him, and I can be so self-conscious. But, I love being around him!

Sometimes I can act normal, and other times I am freaky. As I am listening to him today, I don't even know why but I giggle.

June 27

Okay I didn't think bugs and being outside bothered me, but it wasn't the dead of summer then.

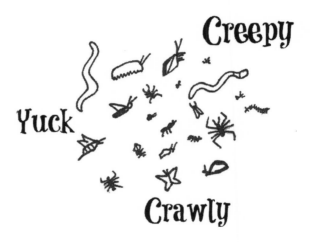

Creepy

Yuck

Crawly

Now that summer has hit...the bugs biting me are AWFUL!!

I put bug spray on, but they still get all over my legs and bite me.

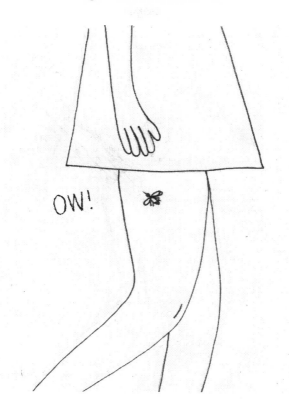

The flies are the worst.

Sometimes, they fly all around me when I am trying to hit the ball.

I have to step away from the ball and start my pre-shot routine over.

A pre-shot routine is a series of steps that you do prior to executing each and every shot. These steps help to develop correct habits that will improve and promote consistency in your golf game. My coach says a good pre-shot routine is the most important part of your mental golf game.

When a bug gets on my leg, it can be so frustrating stepping away from my pre-shot routine and starting all over!

After getting bit by bugs all day, and then trying to sleep at night with them itching, is horrible! Because in my sleep...I SLEEP SCRATCH!

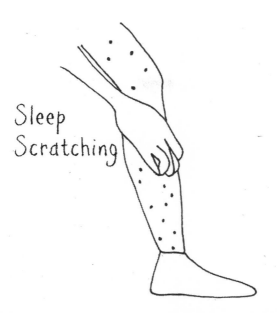

Sleep Scratching

I wake up and my legs look awful!

I don't even know I am doing it.

In the morning there is usually blood on my sheets and scabs all over my legs.

My mom says I look like I have a disease, from ALL the scabs on my legs.

She says she will go onto Google, until her fingers fall off if necessary, but she IS going to find me a bug spray that works (that is not toxic), because my legs look like I am abused.

She said yesterday that someone
asked her at the club what was wrong
with me.

She replied, "Nothing. Why?" They
said they saw my legs and wondered if
I had something wrong with me.

I suggested that she take me to the
salon to get fake fingernails put on.

YES! Fake Nails!!

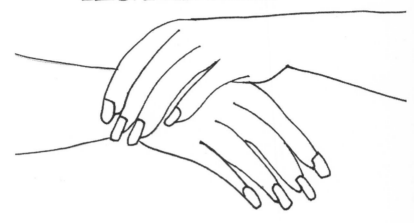

That way I couldn't scratch at night.

She doesn't seem to think this is the best solution. I think it is a GREAT idea!

She didn't even respond to me when I suggested that.

I will give her a few days to let that idea sink in...maybe she will go for it after giving it some thought????

I personally think it is brilliant!! I already know what design I would get on my nails. They would be pink and have a golf theme on them.

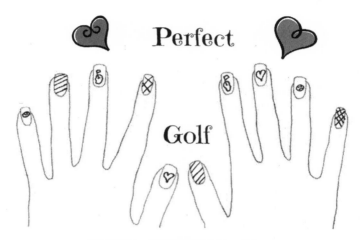

Perfect

Golf

YES PLEASE!!!

So, after all her researching, my mom comes back with a concoction made of essential oils.

She said she has the items in the house and the people online said this one is the best.

She mixes them together and puts them in two different travel spray bottles.

She put one in my golf bag and the other in the house.

I tell her I will try it! I do hope it works. I am tired of the itching!

The recipes is:
Homemade Bug Spray Ingredients needed:

- Essential oils: Citronella, Tea Tree, Eucalyptus,
- Natural Witch Hazel
- Distilled or boiled Water

Homemade Bug Spray Instructions

1. Fill spray bottle (8 ounce) 1/2 full with distilled or boiled water
2. Add witch hazel to fill almost to the top
3. Add 1/2 tsp vegetable glycerin
4. Add 30-50 drops of essential oils to desired scent. The more oils you use, the stronger the spray will be.

If this doesn't work I am going to tell her we tried her idea...now lets try mine.

Fingernails!!!!!

Long beautiful Fake nails!!

I love fake nails because the polish stays on and looks good for weeks. I think this would help my blingtastic look for Tyler!!

NAILS!

BLING!

TYLER!

PERFECTION!!!!!

June 28

My parents are playing in the tournament this weekend for PAW Pals and thought we should practice a captain's choice format before the event on Saturday.

My dad is the longest hitter, and whoever is on his team, in a scramble, is going to have a huge advantage!

Today I was paired with my dad. I loved being his partner and I always learn a lot from him.

It is not necessarily the tee shot today that made the biggest difference, because as a junior player I got a big advantage off the tee.

It was the second shot on a par 5 and the accuracy of his irons into the greens.

One of the biggest lessons I learned was how helpful it is when you put the ball close to the hole.

It was amazing how well we scored.

We also never had a long putt.

It made me realize that a huge key to scoring well is getting the ball close on your approach shot.

My brother had my mom as a partner.

My mom tries, but she is more nurturing on the golf course than she is fierce.

I felt bad for Caleb because he and my mom lost every hole.

We played a 9-hole match, and for 2 hours they took a total beating!

I was having a great time. It is so much fun to win!

It is easy to be upbeat, nice, and happy when you win.

But, they were not having fun being around us, talking to us, or wanting much to do with us!

They were okay when we finished, but Caleb said we were rubbing it in by being so happy.

I felt like we WEREN'T rubbing it in, but I know it is important to have an even personality in golf.

Whether winning or losing to not act excited or sad.

Okay, maybe we were laughing and celebrating a little…too much??

However, this is one of the things I am working on right now.

It really is better for your mental game to remain emotionally neutral whether you have had a good or bad hole.

My coach always says you need to put the last hole behind you if you have a bad hole, but honestly it needs to be the same for a good hole too.

Every time you tee off...you are starting over.

My mom made the point when we got home, that she was so upset she wasn't sure she wanted to play with us again.

She said she learned something...that if it is not fun, you won't continue doing it! It really made her think about how important it is to keep sports fun for kids.

June 29

We have worked so hard and quickly at collecting donations, getting people to sign up, laying out the format, tee times, and rules for today.

I am super excited, and I hope everything goes perfect today!!

I am excited for the event, but I think I am even MORE excited to get to hold MY puppy, and to play with all the other adorable puppies that will be here today and are up for adoption.

As the puppies arrive I run over to the adoption truck to help get the kennels down.

CUTE...BUT NOT BOSTON BABY

ADORABLE...BUT NOT MY BOSTON BABY

SWEET...BUT NOT MY BOSTON BABY

As each kennel gets handed to me I quickly look inside. I am looking for MY little puppy!

My baby Boston Terrier that I fell in love with when I went to volunteer with Tyler.

I keep looking inside every kennel that comes off the truck.

When the last one comes off...I know this has to be the one. I am so excited and smiling so big because I know this is her!

I look inside and my heart immediately sinks.

No baby Boston. :(

An adorable puppy by not my Boston Baby?

I try to not show my disappointment, but I am heartbroken!

I feel like crying!!

I decide to give myself a minute and go check on Putt to distract myself and to keep myself from crying!

I head over to the practice putting green where I set up the raffle. I divided the practice green into squares with chalk.

Each square has a number in it.

It is $5 to buy a number. You can also buy carrots for $1 to place on your square on the green.

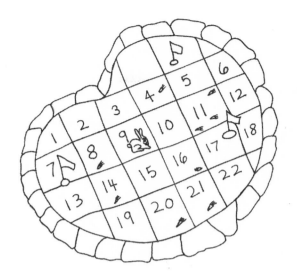

I am really happy Putt gets to participate in today's event.

His name is perfect for this raffle because it is being held on the Putting green.

I make a sign that says WIN A TRIP to Pinehurst for 4!. Buy a raffle ticket!

People can buy a square and see if Putt, the bunny, will land on their square come starting time.

My cute little Putt is just hopping around the practice green.

He looks so happy and takes time to stop and eat a carrot here and there.

I borrowed gates from the shelter to put around the green so Putt wouldn't hop off.

Also, if a puppy got loose Putt wouldn't be in danger.

At 3:00, the time of the shotgun start, whatever numbered square Putt is sitting on, is the winner.

A Shotgun start in a golf tournament is where all groups of players tee off simultaneously from different holes.

The winner of the raffle wins a round of Golf for 4 at Pinehurst!

We got this awesome donation from the Palm Woods Country Club connections.

The club pro loves dogs and hooked us up!!!!!

That means the whole $5 ticket and $1 carrot goes toward saving the shelter.

With a prize this good I am selling tickets left and right.

Most people are buying multiple tickets and tons of carrots. YAY!

The puppies that are up for adoption are placed in playpens, under the trees, at the 1st and 10th tee box.

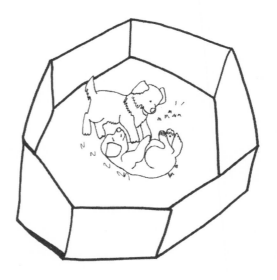

We have a junior player sitting at each location with the playpens set up so everyone can pet and play with the puppies while waiting to tee off.

Each dog has a sign on the outside of its' playpen with a picture and information about it.

I decide to go and look at all the other puppies even though my heart is set on my lost Boston baby puppy.

I just don't understand where she could be?

We have a total of 15 puppies up for adoption today. So far, 6 of them have ADOPTED signs on them.

I know these puppies are going to great homes because golfers are the best!

And, I feel sure we will be able to help Paw Pals stay open.

Tyler comes over to me, smiling, with his hands behind his back.

He said he has been watching me look around and says he can tell I am sad and he can't take it anymore.

Out from behind his back comes MY BOSTON BABY!!!

Here Chloe

I GRAB MY PUPPY AND I BURST INTO TEARS!!!!

I can't believe it...I really thought my puppy was gone.

I asked Tyler, with my voice trembling, "How did you find her?"

He said, "I knew when you saw her the first time that she was YOUR puppy. When the shelter closed I spoke with the owners of Paw Pals and they have been keeping her at their home until today."

They brought her in their car so she wasn't on the adoption truck.

I cannot stop the tears rolling down my face.

Not only did I get my puppy today, but Tyler went through the trouble to save her for me and present her to me.

Through all my tears, in the back of my head, I am thinking...okay...this has to mean something.

He has to be my GBF!!!

Tyler asks, "What are you naming her?"

I look at her sweet, adorable, little face and I immediately reply, "Birdie!"

Tyler has a huge smile on his face, gives a small chuckle and shakes his head.

He says, "I love it!"

I immediately have a thought in my head.

Was it for ME that he went through all this trouble to get me Birdie, or was it for the shelter?

I decide I honestly don't care!!!

Maybe it was a little of both!! The most important thing is...I HAVE MY PUPPY!!!

I carry Birdie, my puppy, around with me for the next 2 hours. I could not set her down. She snuggled right up to my neck.

AWWW
I LOVE HER!!!!

Then she slept in my arms like a baby! I am just so happy!!

The tournament finally finishes up, and all 15 puppies were adopted.

We counted the money we raised and it was a total of $6500 for the shelter.

As a group we are all screaming and jumping up and down when we hear how much money was raised.

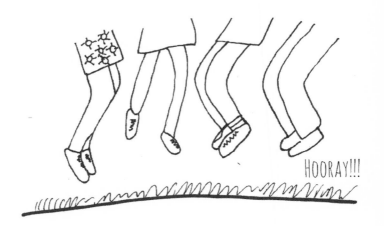

HOORAY!!!

It was 3 times the amount needed for the shelter to stay open.

I love GOLFERS. They are SO GENEROUS!!!

This will not only help the shelter be saved, but there will also be money to buy food and necessary supplies for the dogs.

Today is officially the best day of my life!!

June 30

It has been an AWESOME month!

I got my puppy, helped save the Shelter, and...I officially have a GBF!!! I think??????

SHELTER ✓

BOSTON PUPPY ✓

GBF ?

I can't wait to take Birdie to play golf with me.

I know she is just a puppy, but all I want to do is see if she likes playing golf with me.

I beg my mom to take me to the driving range today with Birdie.

It is late in the evening, and this will be a good test run...before I try to play golf with Birdie in the middle of the day.

We got in the cart, my mom drove, and Caleb and I held her between us in the back.

Birdie

She did okay on the ride, but I had to hold her leash real tight to make her stay beside us.

As soon as we get to the range Birdie starts whining, whimpering, and does a few barks at a man hitting out of the practice bunker.

I make sure I have a tight hold on the leash and get out of the cart with her.

She is pulling and pulling and whining and wants to run after all the golf balls, golfers, and run around on the grass.

SHE IS SO WILD! AND LOUD!!!

I am trying to figure out how I am going to hit golf balls, because she seems to love to put the golf balls in her mouth.

My mom finally says, "Chloe, you and Caleb hit balls and I will hold Birdie on the leash."

I feel bad because my mom was going to practice as well.

She likes to practice when the sun is not pounding us and when it is not as crowded.

But, I really didn't see any other option.

After about 15 min my mom has an idea.

She gets my bag. Sets it WAY behind me.

So that if the leash is fully stretched out it won't reach me, and puts Birdie on the leash.

She starts hitting balls and I think...okay, this is going to work. WRONG!

Birdie is whining and barking and rolling around and twisting up the leash.

I can't even concentrate!

My mom suggests we head home because this just isn't going to work.

Caleb asks, "Can we play the 2 holes on the way to our house?"

My mom says, "We can try. Let's see if Birdie is better while we play than she is while we practice!"

We tee off and we take turns holding Birdie in the cart while we each hit.

So far, so good.

We hit our second shots, and we all are on the green.

Since it is so late at night my mom thought Birdie could be loose and run around while we putt.

As soon as Birdie gets off the leash she runs and picks up my golf ball, with her mouth, on the green and runs off with it.

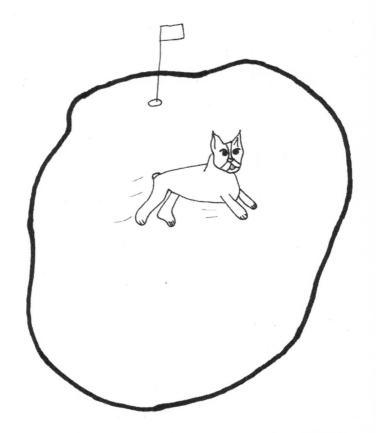

She drops it, runs through the sand trap like a banshee, runs back up, grabs Caleb's ball and runs down the fairway with it.

This is terrible! There is no way this is going to work!

My mom hollers sharply, "I'll get our putters and head to the cart, you two try to catch Birdie!"

Caleb and I run after Birdie.

We are calling her, acting like we have something in our hands to see if we can get her to come over, anything to try to catch her.

Caleb finally caught her with a quick grab.

I put the leash on her and we put her
back in the cart.

We decided to just take her home.
This did NOT go as I had planned!

I see pictures in magazines and on the
Internet where people's dogs will lay
down beside them or sit sweetly while
they play golf.

I may have found the right dog for our family but the wrong dog for behaving while playing golf! UGH!!!

My mom tells me to not be discouraged because she is a puppy. Puppies are not the most obedient.

I am going to work really hard with Birdie and get her to be enjoyable and behave while playing golf with me. It may take me a while, but I now have a new goal!

Golf Training my puppy!

Confused

Smooch

Not Sure

Worried

Uncertain

Happy

Good

Angry

Birdie

About the Author:

Gwen Elizabeth Foddrell is from Richmond, Virginia. She is a true animal lover. She loves to organize, decorate, and do-it-yourself projects. She loves all things girl, like nail polish, heels, and jewelry. She loves the sport of golf and hanging with her family and friends...and of course, she is always up for girl talk!

I want to thank my Mom and Dad for helping me follow my dreams and supporting my love of golf. I want to thank my Brother for giving me good writing material and being my true friend.

Made in the USA
Middletown, DE
14 June 2019